K¹² Classics
for Young Readers

Volume A

Book Staff and Contributors

Kristen Kinney-Haines *Director, Primary Literacy*
Alane Gernon-Paulsen *Content Specialist*
Mary Beck Desmond *Senior Text Editor*
Karen Ingebretsen *Text Editor*
Suzanne Montazer *Creative Director, Print and ePublishing*
Jayoung Cho, Oltjen Design Associates *Print Visual Designers*
Kim Barcas, Stephanie Shaw Williams *Cover Designers*
Susan Raley *Senior Manager, Editors*
Deanna Lacek *Project Manager*

Maria Szalay *Executive Vice President, Product Development*
John Holdren *Senior Vice President, Content and Curriculum*
David Pelizzari *Vice President, Content and Curriculum*
Kim Barcas *Vice President, Creative*
Laura Seuschek *Vice President, Instructional Design, Evaluation & Studies*
Aaron Hall *Vice President, Program Management*

Lisa Dimaio Iekel *Senior Production Manager*
Ray Traugott *Production Manager*

Illustrations Credits

All illustrations © K12 unless otherwise noted

Gynux, 2–9; Monica Guttierez, 10–25; Virginia Allyn, 26–33; Carolina Farías, 34–53; Kathi Ember, 54–67; Jayoung Cho, 68–85; Kristin Sorra, 86–99; Sachiko Yoshikawa, 100–123; John Manders, 124–147; Bandelin-Dacey Studios, 148–173; Valeria Cis, 174–179; Jason Wolff, 180–183; Jayoung Cho, 184–187; Gynux, 188–201; Ian Joven, 202–205; Donald Wu, 206–211; Ian Joven, 212–215; Sarah Schanze, 216–219; Virginia Allyn, 220–223; Peter Francis, 224–233

About K12 Inc.

K12 Inc., a technology-based education company, is the nation's leading provider of proprietary curriculum and online education programs to students in grades K–12. K12 provides its curriculum and academic services to online schools, traditional classrooms, blended school programs, and directly to families. K12 Inc. also operates the K12 International Academy, an accredited, diploma-granting online private school serving students worldwide. K12's mission is to provide any child the curriculum and tools to maximize success in life, regardless of geographic, financial, or demographic circumstances. K12 Inc. is accredited by CITA. More information can be found at www.K12.com.

978-1-60153-207-7
Printed by Worzalla, Stevens Point, WI, USA, April 2016

Contents

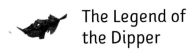

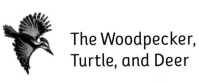

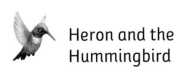 

K^{12} Classics
for Young Readers

Volume A

The *Legend* *of the* Dipper

adapted from J. Berg Esenwein and Marietta Stockard

There had been no rain in the land for a very long time. It was so hot and dry that the flowers were drooping, the grass was parched and brown, and even the big, strong trees were dying. The water dried up in the creeks and the rivers, the wells were dry, and the fountains stopped bubbling. The cows, the dogs, the horses, the birds, and all the people were *so* thirsty! Everyone felt uncomfortable and sick.

There was one little girl whose mother grew very ill. "Oh," said the little girl, "if only I can find some water for my mother, I'm sure she will be well again. I must find some water."

So, she took a tin dipper and started out in search of water. By and by, she found a tiny little spring way up on a mountainside. It was almost dry. The water dripped, dripped, ever so slowly from under the rock. The little girl held her dipper carefully and caught the drops. She waited and waited a long, long time until the dipper was full of water. Then, she started down the mountain holding the dipper very carefully, for she didn't want to spill a single drop.

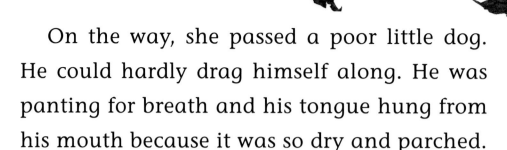

On the way, she passed a poor little dog. He could hardly drag himself along. He was panting for breath and his tongue hung from his mouth because it was so dry and parched.

"Oh, you poor little dog," said the little girl. "You are so thirsty. I can't pass you without giving you a few drops of water. If I give you just a little, there will still be enough for my mother."

So, the little girl poured some water into her hand and held it down for the little dog. He lapped it up quickly, and then he felt so much better that he frisked and barked and almost seemed to say, "Thank you, little girl!" And, although the girl didn't notice, her tin dipper had changed into a silver dipper and was just as full of water as it had been before.

She thought about her mother and hurried along as fast as she could go. When she reached home, it was late in the afternoon, almost dark. The little girl pushed the door open and hurried up to her mother's room. When she

came into the room, the old servant, who had been working hard all day taking care of the sick woman, came to the door. She was so tired and thirsty that she couldn't even speak to the little girl.

"Do give her some water," said the mother. "She has worked hard all day, and she needs it much more than I do."

So, the little girl held the dipper to her lips and the old servant drank some water. She felt stronger and better right away. The little girl didn't notice that the dipper had changed into gold and was just as full of water as before!

Then, she held the dipper to her mother's lips, and her mother drank and drank. Oh, she felt so much better! When she had finished, there was still some water left in the dipper. The little girl was just raising it to her lips when there came a knock at the door. The servant opened it, and there stood a stranger. He was very pale and all covered with dust from traveling. "I am so thirsty," he said. "Won't you please give me a little water?"

The little girl said, "Yes, I will. I am sure you need it more than I do. Drink it all."

The stranger smiled and took the dipper in his hand, and as he took it, it changed into a dipper of pure, bright diamond. He turned it upside down, and all the water spilled out and sank into the ground. And where it spilled, a fountain bubbled up. The cool water flowed and splashed—enough for all the people and animals in the land to have all the water they wanted to drink.

As they watched the water, they forgot the stranger, but presently when they looked, he was gone. They thought they could see him just vanishing in the sky. And there in the sky, clear and high, shone the diamond dipper. It shines up there yet, and its bright glow reminds people of the little girl who was so kind and unselfish. ❧

Medio Pollito:
The Little Half-Chick

Once upon a time, there was a pretty black Spanish hen. Now, this hen had 13 baby chicks. They were all fine, plump little birds—all except one. The youngest chick was quite unlike his brothers and sisters. Indeed, he was a strange, odd-looking creature.

His mother could scarcely believe her eyes when he first chipped his way out of his shell. He was so different from the 12 other fluffy little chicks that nestled under her wings. This one looked as if he had been cut in half. He had only one leg, and one wing, and one eye. He had just half a head and half a beak. So, his mother named him *Medio Pollito*. In Spanish, that means "half-chick."

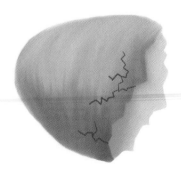
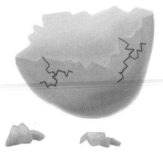

His mother shook her head as she looked at Medio Pollito. She said, "My youngest born is only a half-chick. He can never go out into the world with his brothers and sisters. This poor little fellow must always stay home with his mother."

Medio Pollito looked like an odd, helpless little thing. But, his mother soon found that he was not at all willing to remain under her wing and protection. His brothers and sisters were all good, obedient chickens. When their mother clucked at them, those 12 chicks chirped and ran to her side. But not Medio Pollito! He pretended that he did not hear her clucks and hopped away on his one leg to do just as he pleased.

As Medio Pollito grew older, he became more stubborn and disobedient. He was often rude to his mother and disagreeable to the other chickens.

One day, he had been out roving longer than usual in the fields. On his return, he strutted up to his mother with the peculiar little hop and kick that was his way of walking.

Medio Pollito looked at his mother in a bold way with his one eye and said, "Mother, I am tired of this life in a dull farmyard, with nothing but a dreary field of corn to look at. I'm off to Madrid to see the king."

"To Madrid, Medio Pollito!" exclaimed his mother. "Why, you silly chick, it would be a long journey for a grown-up rooster. A poor little thing like you would be tired out before you had gone half the distance. No, no, stay at home with your mother. Someday, when you are bigger, we might make the journey together."

But, Medio Pollito had made up his mind. He would not listen to his mother's advice, nor to the pleading of his brothers and sisters.

"What is the use of our crowding each

other in this poky little place?" he asked. "When I have a fine courtyard of my own at the king's palace, I might ask some of you to come and pay me a short visit." Then, scarcely waiting to say good-bye to his family, away he hopped down the high road that led to Madrid.

His mother ran after him, calling out, "Be sure that you are kind and polite to everyone you meet." But, he was in such a hurry to be off that he did not wait to answer her. He did not even look back.

A little later, as he was taking a shortcut through a field, he passed a stream. The stream was choked and overgrown with weeds, so its waters could not flow freely.

"Oh! Medio Pollito," it cried, as the half-chick hopped along its banks. "Do come and help me by clearing away these weeds."

"Help you, indeed!" exclaimed Medio Pollito. He tossed his head and shook the few feathers in his tail. "Do you think I have nothing to do but to waste my time? Help yourself, and don't bother busy travelers. I am off to Madrid to see the king." Then, away went Medio Pollito, *hoppity-kick, hoppity-kick*.

A little later, he came to a fire that had been left burning by some travelers in a wood. It was burning very low and would soon be out.

"Oh! Medio Pollito," cried the fire, in a weak, wavering voice as the half-chick approached. "In a few minutes, I shall go quite out, unless you put some sticks and dry leaves upon me. Do help me, or I shall die!"

"Help you, indeed!" answered Medio Pollito. "I have other things to do. Gather sticks for yourself, and don't trouble me. I am off to Madrid to see the king." Then, away went Medio Pollito, *hoppity-kick, hoppity-kick.*

The next morning, as he was getting near Madrid, he passed a large chestnut tree. There, the wind was caught and entangled in the tree's branches. "Oh! Medio Pollito," called the wind. "Please climb up here and help me get free of these branches. I cannot get away, and it is so uncomfortable."

"It's your own fault for going there," answered Medio Pollito. "I can't waste all my morning stopping here to help you. Just shake yourself off, and don't bother me, for I am off to Madrid to see the king." Then, *hoppity-kick, hoppity-kick*, away went Medio Pollito in great glee, for the towers and roofs of Madrid were now in sight.

When he entered the town, he saw before him a great splendid house, with soldiers standing before the gates. He knew that this house must be the king's palace, and he was determined to hop up to the front gate and wait there until the king came out. But as he was hopping past one of the back windows, the king's cook saw him.

"Here is the very thing I want," the cook exclaimed. "For the king has just sent a message to say that he must have chicken broth for his dinner." The cook opened the window and stretched out his arm. He caught Medio Pollito and popped him into the soup pot that was standing near the fire.

MEDIO POLLITO: THE LITTLE H___-CHICK

Oh! How wet and clammy the water felt as it went over Medio Pollito's head. The water made his feathers so wet that they clung to his side. "Water, water!" cried the half-chick. "Have pity upon me, and do not soak me like this."

"Ah! Medio Pollito," replied the water. "You would not help me when I was a little stream away on the fields. Now, you must be punished."

Then, the fire began to burn Medio Pollito. He danced and hopped from one side of the pot to the other, trying to get away from the heat. At last, he cried out, "Fire, fire! Do not burn me like this—it hurts!"

"Ah! Medio Pollito," answered the fire. "You would not help me when I was dying away in the wood. Now, you are being punished."

Medio Pollito thought that he could not stand the burning pain any longer. Then, the cook lifted up the lid of the pot to see if the broth was ready for the king's dinner.

"Look here!" he cried in horror. "This chicken is quite useless. It is burnt to a crisp. I can't send it up to the royal table." So, the cook opened the window and threw Medio Pollito out into the street. But, the wind caught up the half-chick and whirled him through the air so quickly that he could scarcely breathe. Medio Pollito's heart beat against his side till he thought it would break.

"Oh, wind!" he gasped out. "If you hurry me along like this, you will kill me. Do let me rest a moment, or——." He was so breathless that he could not finish his sentence.

MEDIO POLLITO: THE LITTLE HALF-CHICK

MEDIO POLLITO: THE LITTLE HALF-CHICK

"Ah! Medio Pollito," replied the wind. "When I was caught in the branches of the chestnut tree, you would not help me. Now, you are being punished." The wind swirled Medio Pollito over the roofs of the houses till they reached the highest church in the town. There, the wind left the half-chick fastened to the top of the steeple.

And there stands Medio Pollito to this day. If you go to Madrid and walk through the streets till you come to the highest church, you will see the little half-chick. He is perched on his one leg on the steeple. His one wing droops at his side, and he is gazing sadly out of his one eye over the town.

King Midas

Once upon a time, there lived a very rich king, whose name was Midas. This king was very fond of gold. He loved it more than anything in the world.

King Midas had a little daughter named Marygold. When Marygold picked buttercups and dandelions, he used to say, "If these flowers were as golden as they look, I would pick them."

One day, King Midas was in his treasure room counting his treasure. He looked up and saw a stranger in the room.

"You are a rich man, friend Midas," said the stranger.

"Yes, I have some gold," answered Midas. "But, it is not enough."

"What!" cried the stranger. "Are you not happy?"

Midas shook his head.

"What would make you happy? What do you wish?"

King Midas thought and thought. At last, he looked at the stranger and said, "I wish that everything I touch may turn to gold."

"Are you sure you would be happy then?"

"Yes," answered Midas. "I would ask for nothing more."

"It shall be as you wish," said the stranger. "Tomorrow at sunrise, you shall have the Golden Touch."

When the sun peeped into the room, King Midas jumped out of bed.

He touched a chair. It turned to gold.

He touched the bed and the table, and they were changed to solid, shining gold.

He dressed himself, and all his clothes were gold.

Then, King Midas went into his garden. "Now," he thought, "I can have the most beautiful garden in the world."

So, he touched all the leaves and flowers, and they became shining gold.

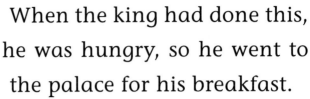

When the king had done this, he was hungry, so he went to the palace for his breakfast.

He tried to drink some water. When he touched it to his lips, it turned into gold. He touched the fish on his plate. It became a pretty gold fish, and he could not eat it.

He took an egg. That, too, turned into gold.

Just then, Marygold ran to her father and put her arms about his neck. "Good morning, dear Father," she said.

The king kissed his little daughter. "My dear, dear Marygold," he cried. But, Marygold did not answer.

Alas! What had he done! His dear daughter, his sweet little Marygold, was changed to gold by his kiss.

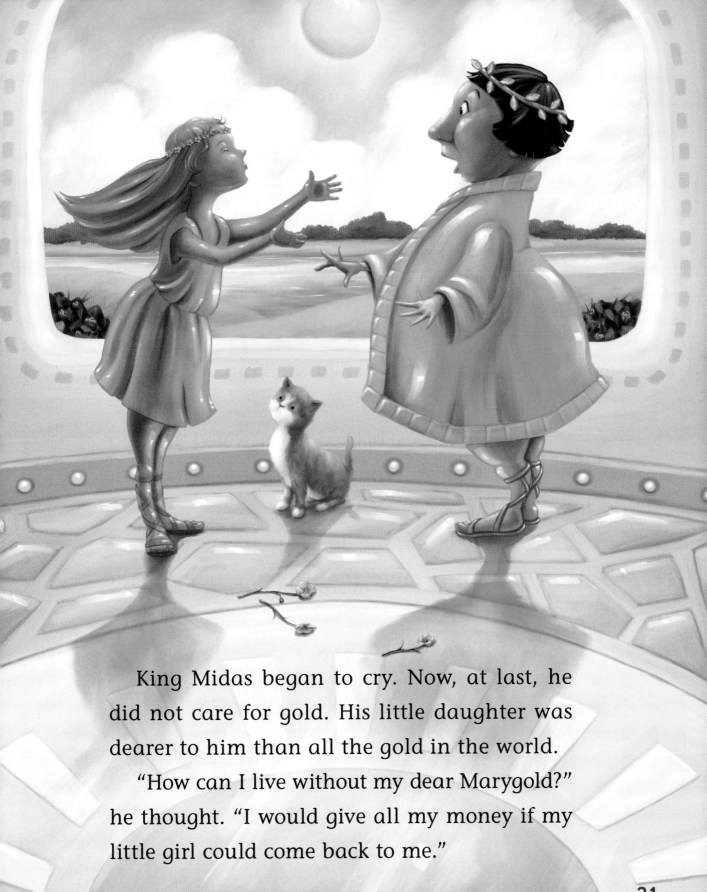

King Midas began to cry. Now, at last, he did not care for gold. His little daughter was dearer to him than all the gold in the world.

"How can I live without my dear Marygold?" he thought. "I would give all my money if my little girl could come back to me."

Then, the stranger came again. "Well, friend Midas," he said, "how do you like the Golden Touch?"

"I am very unhappy," said Midas. "I know now that gold is not everything."

"Let us see," said the stranger. "Which do you think is worth more—the Golden Touch, or a cup of water?"

"A cup of water!" cried the king.

"The Golden Touch, or a crust of bread?"

"Give me a crust of bread," answered the king.

"The Golden Touch, or your dear little Marygold?"

"Oh, my child, my dear child!" cried Midas. "She is worth more than all the gold in the world."

"Go, then, to the river at the foot of your garden," said the stranger. "The water in the river will take away the Golden Touch. Fill this pitcher with the water, and sprinkle everything you have touched."

King Midas ran through the garden and jumped into the river.

Then, he filled the pitcher and ran back to the palace. He sprinkled the water over the golden child, and she became his own little laughing, dancing Marygold once more. ❧

Strong Wind's Bride

a legend from the Algonquian Indians

Once upon a time, in a beautiful wigwam on the shores of a broad lake, there lived a mighty warrior. Not only was he strong and brave, but he also had the power to make himself invisible, like the wind—and so he was called Strong Wind. No one had ever seen Strong Wind but his sister. He brought her many deer and supplied her with good things to eat from the forest and lake, and with the finest blankets and garments. But when visitors came, all they ever saw of Strong Wind were his moccasins. For when he took them off, they became visible, and his sister hung them up.

One spring day, Strong Wind's sister walked along the shore of the lake to the nearby village. There, she made an announcement to the people: "You all know of my brother, Strong Wind, who is kind and brave, but invisible to all eyes except my own. He has decided that the time has come for him to marry. He will marry the girl who can see him and tell me his true appearance."

After that, every day at sunset, many girls walked along the lakeshore to Strong Wind's wigwam, where they found his sister waiting. And as Strong Wind came home in the twilight, pulling behind him a sled piled with deer or other animals from the hunt, she asked, "Do you see my brother?"

And, some of the girls said, "No." But, many answered, "Yes, I see him."

"If you can see him," said the sister, "then tell me, what does he use to pull his sled?"

And, one girl would answer, "A strip of rawhide," while another would say, "A strong cord."

Then, Strong Wind's sister knew they had lied, and she sent them home, for Strong Wind would not marry one who was untruthful.

Now, in the village by the lake, there lived a poor man who had three daughters. The youngest daughter was kind, gentle, and loved by all. But, the older two were jealous, and they treated her very cruelly. They gave her only rags to wear, cut off her braids, and forced her to work over the fire, so that the sparks burned her hands and face.

"Now, who will want to marry you, you ugly burnt-faced girl!" they cackled, and the young girl hid her face in her hands and wept.

One day, the elder sisters put on their finest clothes, braided their hair, and draped themselves with necklaces and bracelets. Together, they strutted along the lakeshore to meet Strong Wind's sister, in hopes of marrying the mighty warrior.

Soon, Strong Wind returned from his day's hunting, and his sister asked the girls, "Do you see my brother?"

"Of course, we see him," they replied.

"If you can see him, then tell me, what does he use to pull his sled?"

"He uses a cord made from the hide of a moose," they said.

At once, Strong Wind's sister knew they had lied. "Very well," she said softly. "Let us return to the wigwam."

The girls helped Strong Wind's sister cook the evening meal. As they finished cooking, the door of the wigwam moved to one side. Then, as the girls watched in amazement, they saw the supper they had prepared disappear bite by bite. Then, they watched as the sister held out her hands and took a pair of moccasins that seemed to float in midair, and hung them up. After that, the girls neither saw nor heard anything more, and they went home in shame.

"It's not fair!" they whined. "No one can see him!"

"Perhaps, I will," said the youngest sister. The elder girls laughed at her and called her a fool. "And, even if you did see him," they cried, "do you think he would ever marry you, with your scarred face and chopped-off braids?" But, the youngest sister said nothing, and went patiently about her work.

In the afternoon, the burnt-faced girl walked deep into the woods and gathered strips of white bark from the birch trees. She sewed the pieces of bark together to make a dress and a cap. And on them, she carved pictures of birds and beasts; flowers and trees; and the sun, the moon, and the stars. Then, she put on a pair of her father's old, worn-out moccasins, for she had no other shoes to wear.

As she made her way along the lake, her sisters saw her and laughed. "Go home!" they shrieked. "Strong Wind will never marry an ugly girl like you. Go home!"

But, when Strong Wind's sister met the girl, she smiled and said, "Welcome. Will you come with me to greet my brother?"

Together, they walked to where the trees of the forest met the waters of the lake. And, as the sun set, Strong Wind's sister asked, "Do you see him?"

But, the girl answered sadly, "No, I do not see him."

Strong Wind's sister smiled again, because the girl had told the truth. A few moments later, she asked, "Do you see him now?"

The girl gazed out through the twilight. Suddenly, she cried, "Oh, I do see him! I do! And, he is wonderful."

"Tell me," said his sister, "what does he use to pull his sled?"

"He pulls his sled with the rainbow."

The sister's eyes lit up. "And, can you tell me," she asked, "of what is his bowstring made?"

"His bowstring," said the burnt-faced girl, her voice filled with wonder, "is the Milky Way, the wide road of stars that stretches across the sky."

Then, Strong Wind's sister said, "Surely, my brother has looked past your burnt, scarred face and seen your beautiful, gentle heart, for he has made himself visible to you. You have seen him, and spoken truly."

Then, she took the girl by the hand and led her to the wigwam, and bathed her with cool, clear dew, until the burns and scars all disappeared from her body and face. Her skin became smooth and soft, and her hair grew long and black again, like a raven's wing. Then, Strong Wind's sister gave the girl a beautiful dress and a necklace of porcupine quills to wear, and invited her to sit in the bride's seat in the wigwam.

When Strong Wind entered, he smiled at her and said, "So, we have found each other at last."

And, she simply answered, "Yes—at last."

The very next day, she became his wife, and they lived ever afterward in great happiness. ❧

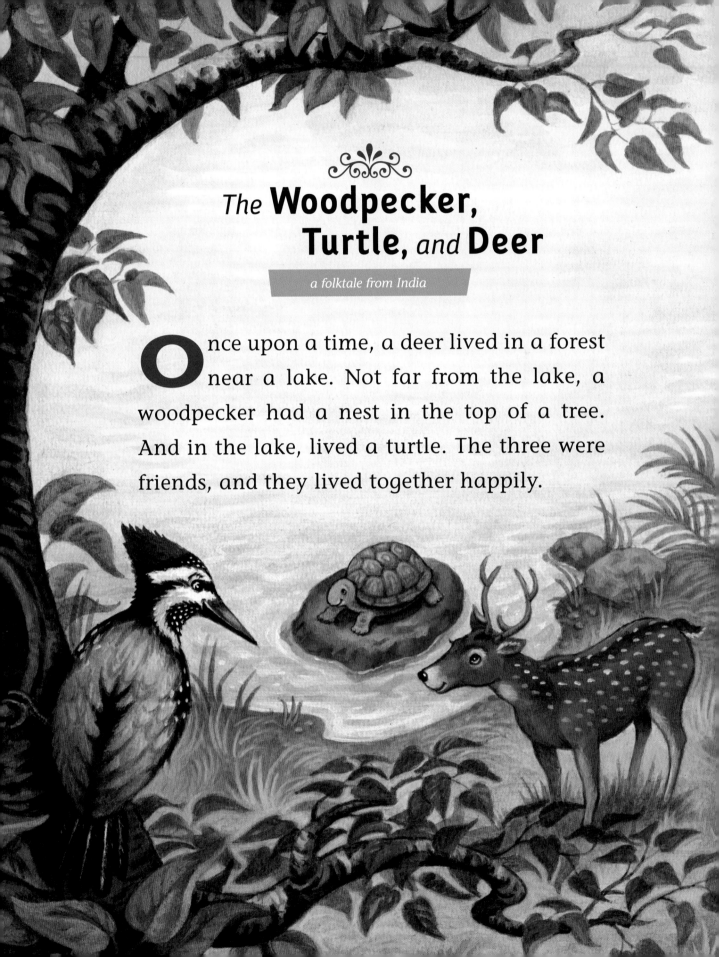

The **Woodpecker, Turtle,** and **Deer**

a folktale from India

Once upon a time, a deer lived in a forest near a lake. Not far from the lake, a woodpecker had a nest in the top of a tree. And in the lake, lived a turtle. The three were friends, and they lived together happily.

One day, a hunter wandering about in the wood saw the footprints of the deer near the edge of the lake. "I will trap this deer when it goes down to the water to drink," he said. He set a strong trap of leather and went on his way.

Early that night, when the deer went down to drink, he was caught in the trap. He cried out for help.

At once, the woodpecker flew down from the treetop, and the turtle came out of the water to see what could be done.

Said the woodpecker to the turtle, "Friend, you have sharp teeth. Use them to gnaw through the leather trap. I will go and see to it that the hunter keeps away. If we both do our best, our friend will not lose his life."

So, the turtle began to gnaw the leather, and the woodpecker flew to the hunter's house.

At dawn, the hunter came, knife in hand, to the front door of his house.

The woodpecker, flapping her wings, flew at the hunter and struck him in the face.

The hunter turned back into the house and lay down for a little while. Then, he rose up again and took his knife. He said to himself, "When I went out by the front door, a bird flew in my face. This time, I will go out by the back door."

But, the woodpecker thought, "The hunter went out by the front door before, so now he will leave by the back door." So, the woodpecker perched in a tree near the back door.

When the hunter came out, the bird flew at him again, flapping her wings in the hunter's face. Then, the hunter turned back and ran inside. After a while, he took his knife and started out once more.

The woodpecker flew back as fast as she could fly to her friends, crying, "Hurry! Hurry! Here comes the hunter!"

By this time, the turtle had gnawed through all the pieces of the trap but one. The leather was so hard that it made his teeth feel as if they would fall out, and his poor gums were bleeding. The deer heard the woodpecker, and he saw the hunter, knife in hand, coming on.

With a strong pull, the deer broke the last piece of the trap and ran into the woods.

The woodpecker flew up to her nest in the treetop. But, the turtle was so weak that he could not get away. He lay where he was. The hunter picked him up and threw him into a bag, tying it to a tree.

The deer saw that the turtle had been taken, and he made up his mind to save his friend's life. So, the deer let the hunter see him.

The hunter seized his knife and started after the deer. The deer, keeping just out of his reach, led the hunter deeper and deeper into the forest.

When the deer saw that they had gone far into the forest, he slipped away from the hunter, and swift as the wind, he went by another way to where he had left the turtle.

But, the turtle was not there. The deer called, "Turtle, Turtle!"

The turtle called out, "Here I am in this bag, hanging from a tree."

Then, the deer lifted the bag with his antlers and placed it on the ground. He tore the bag open and let the turtle out.

The woodpecker flew down from her nest, and the deer said to them, "You two friends saved my life, but if we stay here talking, the hunter will find us, and we may not get away. So, friend Woodpecker, fly away. And you, friend Turtle, dive into the water. I will hide in the forest."

Soon, the hunter did come back, and he saw not a trace of the deer, nor the turtle, nor the woodpecker. He found his torn bag, and picking it up, he gave a frustrated grunt and went back to his home.

As for the three friends, they lived happily together all the rest of their lives. ❧

Stone Soup

a French folktale

Once upon a time, there was a war in a far-off land. When the war ended, the people were tired after many years of fighting. And, they were hungry, too, for there was little food left in the land. The people carefully guarded what little food they had, and they even began to hide it from their friends and neighbors.

At this time, a soldier was coming home from the war. He had walked long and far, and he was tired and hungry. He saw a village ahead. "Ah," he thought. "Perhaps here I can rest. And, if the villagers are kind, they will offer me a little food and drink."

But, as the soldier approached the village, he saw the people scurrying into their houses and slamming their doors behind them. "Hmm," muttered the soldier, "that's an odd way to welcome a weary traveler."

He walked up to the first house and knocked on the door. "Good evening!" he called out. "I've been walking a long way, and I'm hungry and cold. I seek a bite to eat and a place to sleep tonight."

"Just keep walking!" cried a voice from inside. "We have hardly enough food for ourselves, and nothing to share."

The soldier sighed and knocked on the next door. "Good evening!" he called. "I have been walking long and am hungry and cold."

"Go away!" cried a voice from inside. "There's hardly a bite to eat in all the land, and certainly none to spare."

The soldier knocked at every door, but no one would let him in or give him even a morsel of food. So, he walked to the square at the center of the village, and there he stopped. He patted each of his many pockets, as though searching for something important. Then, he gave a great smile and announced in a loud voice, "Ah, here it is!" as he pulled a smooth, round stone from one of his pockets. "After all," he said, "I have all that I need, for I can make a nice big pot of stone soup."

One old woman, who had cracked open her door to watch the soldier, cried, "I've never heard of such a thing! How can you make soup from a stone?"

"Bring me a kettle," said the soldier, "and you will see."

The old woman brought out a small, rusty pot. The soldier shook his head and said, "Thank you, but I will need a bigger pot if I am going to cook for the whole village."

"For the *whole village*?" exclaimed the old woman. She hobbled across the square and banged on one of the heavy doors. "Open the door!" she cried. "Lend us your kettle! This soldier says he can make soup from a stone, enough for the whole village."

A moment later, a man and his two strong sons lumbered out the door, carrying an enormous kettle between them. When they had dragged it to the center of the square, the soldier said, "Thank you. Now, I must have water to fill the kettle and a good, hot fire to heat the water."

One by one, the curious villagers left their houses and formed a line from the well to the square. They passed buckets of water from hand to hand to fill the kettle. They piled logs under the kettle and built a roaring fire. Then, they crowded around the soldier and watched as he carefully dropped the stone into the kettle and began to stir.

After a little while, he dipped a spoon into the kettle and tasted a small sip. "Ahhh!" he exclaimed. "It's good, very good indeed. But if

I had just a pinch of salt and a dash of pepper, it would be even better."

"I might have a grain or two left in my cupboard," a woman said. She ran home, and when she returned, she dropped a fistful of salt and a cup of pepper into the boiling water.

"Imagine," she said, "soup made from a stone!"

"Thank you," said the soldier. "Now, if we had a carrot and perhaps a potato or two, I could make this soup truly delicious."

"Surely we have a carrot or a potato left in our garden," a man said. He ran home and returned with an armful of carrots and a sack of potatoes.

"And, see here!" cried the soldier. "Your neighbor has also brought an onion the size of the moon!"

The villagers laughed, and one or two patted the man on the back. The man chopped the vegetables, dropped them into the boiling water, and said, "Imagine, soup made from a stone!"

The soldier took another taste of the soup. "Marvelous!" he cried. "Now, if only we had a bit of beef and barley, this soup would be fit for a king."

Immediately, some villagers ran home and returned with a side of beef and a sack of barley.

The soldier stirred in the ingredients, and a rich aroma soon filled the air. He took a taste, closed his eyes, and smiled.

Just then, a small child with bright red hair approached. She looked up at the soldier with shy eyes. Then, she held out a plump green cabbage.

"Perfect!" cried the soldier. He bent to thank the child and placed a gentle kiss on her red hair.

As the soldier chopped the cabbage into the kettle, the villagers cried, "Stone soup! We want stone soup!"

"There is enough for everyone," replied the soldier. "Let us set a table and eat together."

The men carried out benches and long wooden tables. The women spread the tables with cloths and brought out spoons. The children gathered flowers and set a bouquet in the center of each table. Then, they hurried home to change into their best clothes.

"Come now," said a man to the soldier. "My oldest son is about your size. Let us see if we can find you a better suit of clothes."

So, the soldier went home with the man and was given a fine set of new clothes. When he returned to the square, he ladled out the soup until all were served. Then, they ate and drank until they were full, and the villagers whispered, "Imagine! Who knew that stone soup could be so delicious?"

In good cheer, they told stories and sang songs. One brought out a fiddle, another played a flute, and they danced until the stars came out.

At last, it was time to go to bed. "Is there a barn or a cowshed where I might sleep?" asked the soldier.

"Nonsense!" said the mayor of the village. "You will sleep in my house. We always have room for friends." So, the soldier slept in a soft bed in a warm room.

The next morning, the soldier gathered his things and pushed open the front door. All the villagers had gathered in the square. "Please take this," they said, handing him a bag stuffed with bread and cheese. "It is our way of thanking you for sharing the secret of how to make stone soup."

"I thank you with all my heart," said the soldier. "But, there is no secret but this—even in the hardest times, if each and every one will give a little, then much good can be done for many."

He took the stone from his pocket and placed it in the hands of the red-haired child. Then, whistling a merry tune, he walked down the road, over a hill, and out of sight.

Budulinek

a folktale from Czechoslovakia retold by Parker Fillmore

There was once a little boy named Budulinek. He lived with his old granny in a cottage near a forest.

Granny went out to work every day. In the morning, when she went away, she always said, "There, Budulinek, there's your dinner on the table and mind, you mustn't open the door, no matter who knocks!"

One morning, Granny said, "Now, Budulinek, today I'm leaving you some soup for your dinner. Eat it when dinnertime comes. And, remember what I always say: Don't open the door, no matter who knocks." She went away, and pretty soon Lishka, the sly old mother fox, came and knocked on the door.

"Budulinek!" she called. "You know me! Open the door! Please!"

Budulinek called back, "No, I mustn't open the door."

But, Lishka, the sly old mother fox, kept on knocking. "Listen, Budulinek," she said. "If you open the door, do you know what I'll do? I'll give you a ride on my tail!"

Now, Budulinek thought to himself, "Oh, that would be fun to ride on the tail of Lishka, the fox!"

So, Budulinek forgot all about what Granny said to him every day and opened the door. Lishka, the sly old thing, came into the room, and what do you think she did? Do you think she gave Budulinek a ride on her tail? Well, she didn't. She just went over to the table and gobbled up the bowl of soup that Granny had put there for Budulinek's dinner, and then she ran away.

When dinnertime came, Budulinek hadn't anything to eat.

In the evening, when Granny came home, she said, "Budulinek, did you open the door and let anyone in?"

Budulinek was crying because he was so hungry, and he said, "Yes, I let in Lishka, the sly old mother fox, and she ate up all my dinner, too!"

Granny said, "Now, Budulinek, you see what happens when you open the door and let someone in. Next time, do what Granny says and don't open the door."

The next morning, Granny cooked some porridge for Budulinek's dinner and said, "Now, Budulinek, here's some porridge for your dinner. Remember, while I'm gone, you must not open the door, no matter who knocks."

Granny was no sooner out of sight than Lishka came again and knocked on the door.

"Oh, Budulinek!" she called. "Open the door and let me in!"

But, Budulinek said, "No, I won't open the door!"

"Oh, now, Budulinek, please open the door!" Lishka begged. "You know me! Do you know what I'll do if you open the door? I'll give you a ride on my tail! Truly, I will!"

Budulinek thought, "This time, maybe she will give me a ride on her tail." So, he opened the door. Lishka came into the room, gobbled up Budulinek's porridge, and ran away without giving him any ride at all.

When dinnertime came, Budulinek hadn't anything to eat.

In the evening when Granny came home, she said, "Budulinek, did you open the door and let anyone in?"

Budulinek was crying again because he was so hungry, and he said, "Yes, I let in Lishka, the sly old mother fox, and she ate up all my porridge!"

"Budulinek, you're a bad boy!" Granny said. "If you open the door again, I'll have to punish you! Do you hear?"

The next morning, before she went to work, Granny cooked some peas for Budulinek's dinner. As soon as Granny was gone, he began eating the peas, they were so good.

Presently, Lishka came and knocked on the door.

"Budulinek!" she called. "Open the door! I want to come in!"

But, Budulinek wouldn't open the door. He took his bowl of peas and went to the window and ate them there, where Lishka could see him.

"Oh, Budulinek!" Lishka begged. "You know me! Please open the door! This time, I promise you I'll give you a ride on my tail! Truly, I will!"

She just begged and begged, until at last Budulinek opened the door. Then, Lishka jumped into the room, and do you know what she did? She put her nose right into the bowl of peas and gobbled up the rest!

Then, she said to Budulinek, "Now, get on my tail, and I'll give you a ride!"

So, Budulinek climbed on Lishka's tail, and Lishka went running around the room faster and faster, until Budulinek was dizzy and just had to hold on with all his might.

Then, before Budulinek knew what was happening, Lishka slipped out of the house and ran off swiftly into the forest, home to her hole, with Budulinek still on her tail! She hid Budulinek down in her hole with her own three children, and she wouldn't let him out. He had to stay there with the three little foxes, and they all teased him and nipped at him. And then, wasn't he sorry he had disobeyed his granny! And, oh, how he cried!

When Granny came home, she found the door open and no little Budulinek anywhere. She looked high and low, but no, there was no little Budulinek. She asked everyone she met if they had seen her little Budulinek, but nobody had. So, poor Granny just cried and cried, she was so lonely and sad.

One day, an organ-grinder with a wooden leg began playing in front of Granny's cottage. The music made her think of Budulinek.

"Organ-grinder," Granny said, "here's a penny for you. But, please, don't play any more. Your music makes me cry."

"Why does it make you cry?" the organ-grinder asked.

"Because, it reminds me of Budulinek," Granny said, and she told the organ-grinder all about Budulinek and how somebody had stolen him away.

The organ-grinder said, "Poor Granny! I'll tell you what I'll do. As I go around and play my organ, I'll keep my eyes open for Budulinek. If I find him, I'll bring him back to you."

"Will you?" Granny cried. "If you bring me back my little Budulinek, I'll give you a measure of rye and a measure of millet and a measure of poppy seed and a measure of everything in the house!"

So, the organ-grinder went off, and everywhere he played his organ, he looked for Budulinek. But, he couldn't find him.

At last, one day while he was walking through the forest, he thought he heard a little boy crying. He looked around everywhere until he found a fox hole.

"Oho!" he said to himself. "I believe that wicked old Lishka must have stolen Budulinek! She's probably keeping him here with her own three children! I'll soon find out."

So, he put down his organ and began to play. And as he played, he sang softly:

One old fox
And two, three, four,
And Budulinek
He makes one more!

Old Lishka heard the music playing, and she said to her oldest child, "Here, son, give the old man a penny and tell him to go away because my head aches."

So, the oldest little fox climbed out of the hole and gave the organ-grinder a penny and said, "My mother says, please will you go away because her head aches."

As the organ-grinder reached over to take the penny, he caught the oldest little fox and stuffed him into a sack. Then, he went on playing and singing:

> *One old fox*
> *And two and three*
> *And Budulinek*
> *Makes four for me!*

Presently, Lishka sent out her second child with a penny, and the organ-grinder caught the second little fox in the same way and stuffed him also into the sack. Then, he went on grinding his organ and softly singing:

> *One old fox*
> *And another for me,*
> *And Budulinek*
> *He makes the three.*

"I wonder why that old man still plays his organ," Lishka said, and sent out her third child with a penny.

So, the organ-grinder caught the third little fox and stuffed him also into the sack. Then, he kept on playing and singing softly:

One old fox—
I'll soon get you!—
And Budulinek
He makes just two.

At last, Lishka herself came out. So, he caught her, too, and stuffed her in with her children. Then, he sang:

Four naughty foxes
Caught alive!
And Budulinek
He makes the five!

The organ-grinder went to the hole and called down, "Budulinek! Budulinek! Come out!"

As there were no foxes left to hold him back, Budulinek was able to crawl out.

When he saw the organ-grinder, he cried and said, "Oh, please, Mr. Organ-Grinder, I want to go home to my granny!"

"I'll take you home to your granny," the organ-grinder said. "But first, I must deal with these naughty foxes."

The organ-grinder made the foxes promise that they would never again do anything to Budulinek. Then, he let them go, and he took Budulinek home to Granny.

Granny was delighted to see her little Budulinek, and she gave the organ-grinder a measure of rye and a measure of millet and a measure of poppy seed and a measure of everything else in the house.

And, Budulinek never again opened the door! ∂

Issun Boshi

a folktale from Japan

Once upon a time in a village in Japan, there lived an old man and his wife. They were good and kind, but they were also lonely, because they did not have a child. Every day, they wished and prayed for a child, even one as small as a fingertip.

In time, their wish came true. A child was born to the old man and woman, a baby boy no larger than his father's thumb. The old man and woman cradled the tiny boy in their hands and named him *Issun Boshi*, or "One-Inch Boy."

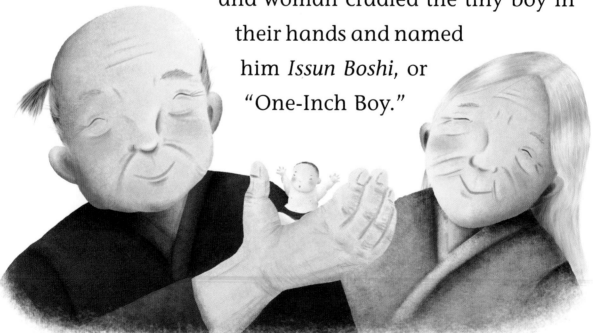

Though Issun Boshi never grew any taller, as he got older, he grew brave and wise. One day, he bowed to his parents and said, "Father and Mother, I ask that you give me your permission to go the great city. I am a young man now, and it is time for me to see the world, to make a name for myself, and to bring honor to our family."

His parents' eyes shone with pride, and they agreed to let him go.

"But, my son must look his best when he goes to the capital city," thought the old woman. So, from a scrap of silk, she made him a new kimono.

"And, my son must have a sword to stand among the warriors," said the old man. So, he made him a sword from a silver sewing needle, and a scabbard from a golden piece of straw.

When the day came for Issun Boshi to set off upon his journey, he put on the new kimono and belted the sword and scabbard at his side. His father and mother gave him a shiny black rice bowl to use as a boat and a chopstick for an oar. Issun Boshi stepped into his boat and used the chopstick to push himself into the river. As he paddled away, he could hear his parents cry, "*Sayonara*, Issun Boshi! Good luck, dear son!"

For many days, he paddled, until one morning he saw the roofs of the great city of Kyoto gleaming in the sun. He quickly steered his boat to shore and climbed out. Then, he pushed the boat back into the river and watched it drift away.

"I will not need that boat again," he said. "When I return to the village, I will travel in a fine carriage." He tightened his straw belt around his waist and marched proudly through the gates of Kyoto.

ISSUN BOSHI

Issun Boshi had never seen any place so busy as Kyoto's main street. "It's a forest of legs! It's a sea of feet!" he cried, as he darted around hurrying sandals and plodding hooves. Carefully, he made his way to the largest, most beautiful house in the city. The lord of the house was standing on the front steps.

"Hello!" shouted Issun Boshi.

"Who is there?" answered the lord of the house. He looked around, but he did not see anyone.

"It is I, Issun Boshi. Here I am, beside your shoes!"

The lord bent down and peered at Issun Boshi. Issun Boshi bowed politely and said, "I have come from my parents' village to work for a great lord and make a name for myself."

The lord nodded and picked up Issun Boshi. "You speak well, Issun Boshi, but I do not know what work a fellow as small as you could do."

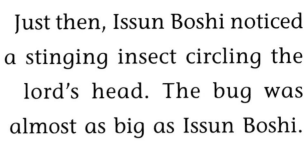

Just then, Issun Boshi noticed a stinging insect circling the lord's head. The bug was almost as big as Issun Boshi. Its stinger was as long as his arm. But, without waiting a moment, Issun Boshi drew his sword and felled the insect with one swift stroke.

The lord stroked his beard and said, "You may be small, but you have great courage. You may come and work for me."

From that day on, Issun Boshi lived in the beautiful house and worked for the lord and his family. He polished the shoes, chased the mice and insects, and stood on the lord's papers while he wrote so they would not blow away in the breeze.

So polite and helpful was he that everyone liked him, especially the lord's fair daughter, the princess. Often, when his day's work was done, he would sit on her shoulder and talk with her as she walked through the gardens, leaping down now and again to clear the pebbles from her path.

Then, one day, Issun Boshi went with the princess and some of her friends and servants to a cherry blossom festival. As they were walking home, a fierce monster, called an *oni*, jumped out from the shadows, roaring and snarling. The princess's servants shrieked and ran away. But, Issun Boshi stood in front of the princess and faced the oni.

"Come no closer, you beast!" he shouted. "Run away while you can!"

"Ha ha!" snarled the oni. "You are funny, little man. I think I will eat you first!"

Then, the oni grabbed Issun Boshi and lifted him up to his mouth. But, Issun Boshi broke free of the oni's grasp and jumped onto the beast's huge nose. He drew his sword and began stabbing at the oni. The oni cried out and clawed at his eyes and face, but Issun Boshi nimbly danced among the monster's fingers, always stabbing with his tiny sword.

"Enough! Enough!" screeched the oni. "I will go away if only you will stop!"

At once, Issun Boshi dropped to the ground, and the oni ran back into the forest, whimpering and crying.

Issun Boshi hurried to the princess. "Look!" she cried. "The oni left behind his magic hammer. It is said," she whispered, "that if you hold this hammer, you may wish for anything you want, and you will receive it."

Issun Boshi replied politely, "Princess, you should make the wish."

But, the princess shook her head. "You were brave. You scared away the oni. You should make the first wish."

Issun Boshi bowed and touched the hammer. "My wish has already been granted, because I serve you and your family. But, if I could make a second wish, I would wish to be as tall as other men."

Suddenly, it seemed to Issun Boshi that the world was shrinking. The rocks by the road no longer looked like mountains. The grass brushed his ankles instead of his shoulders. And, instead of looking at the princess's sandals, he was looking into her eyes.

Then, the princess made a silent wish of her own on the magic hammer, and the two walked quietly back to the beautiful house in Kyoto. The princess told her father how Issun Boshi had fought the oni and saved her life. Her father told the other lords of the city. Soon, the brave young man's story was being told all across Kyoto, and then all across Japan. The emperor himself heard the story. He called Issun Boshi before him and gave him a great reward for his courage.

Not long after, a fine carriage rolled into a village. A tall, handsome young warrior stepped out and knocked on the door of the cottage where an old man and woman lived. "Issun Boshi—is it you?" the old man and woman cried.

"Yes, yes, it is our dear son!" And, they embraced him and cried tears of joy. Then, they packed their belongings and climbed into the carriage to join him.

When they returned to Kyoto, Issun Boshi and the princess were married—and so *her* wish was granted, too. And, together with their parents, they all lived happily for the rest of their days.

The **Poor Man's Reward**

a folktale from West Africa

Long ago, on the wide plains of Africa, there lived a young man who was poor and all alone, for his parents had died, and he owned nothing but the clothes on his back.

One day, the poor man decided he would set off—it didn't matter where—to see if he'd have better luck in another part of the country.

He packed a small amount of meat and millet in a bag, and he filled a small gourd with honey and a large gourd with water. Very early, he set off toward the rising sun.

He walked for miles across the dusty plain, and by the middle of the day, he was hot and tired. As the sun climbed higher in the sky, the sweat rolled down his face, and he wondered if he ought to give up.

Luckily, there was a tree nearby, so he sat under it and rested in the shade. Feeling hungry, he opened his bag and took out some of the millet wrapped in a cloth. Just then, he heard a voice above him.

"I'm starving. Could I have some of your millet?"

He looked up, and there was a weaverbird perched on a branch. It looked thin and worn out. Amazed that the bird could talk, the man replied, "Of course, take as much as you want." And, he held out the millet so that the bird could peck at the grain.

The weaverbird ate its fill, and then it chirped and spread its wings. As it flew away, it cried, "Thank you, my friend. I won't forget your kindness."

The man ate the rest of the millet and went on his way. He walked until dark, and then he climbed into a tree to sleep.

The next day, he walked until midday, and then once more he sat down in the shade of a tree to shelter himself from the burning sun. This time, he thought he would eat the meat, but just as he was pulling it out of his bag, he heard something scratching the ground behind him. He looked around, and there was a scrawny-looking hyena eyeing the meat.

THE POOR MAN'S REWARD

"Excuse me," it said, "but do you think you could spare the bones when you've finished the meat? You see, I haven't eaten for two days."

The man could hardly believe his eyes. Here was a hyena, standing right beside him and talking politely. "Certainly," said the man. "I'll just take a bite or two, and you can have the rest." He took a bite, and then gave the bone, still heavy with meat, to the hyena. The hyena chewed the meat in a few gulps, and then it settled down to gnaw the bone. The man stood up to go.

"Oh—I beg your pardon!" said the hyena. "I was enjoying my meal so much that I nearly forgot to thank you. But, I won't forget your kindness."

The man walked along, his feet sore and his face burning from the heat of the sun. In the evening, he found a tree to sleep in, and the next morning, he started off early, with only the gourds of honey and water left.

At noon, his legs were aching, and he sat down to rest by some bushes. He took the small gourd filled with honey, dipped his fingers in, and scooped some out. He was just about to help himself to more when he heard something buzzing around his head. A tiny voice said, "I'd love some of that. There are no flowers for miles around."

It was a bee. This time, the man wasn't surprised to hear an animal talking. He felt sorry for the hungry creature and immediately held out the gourd so that it could help itself.

The bee ate its fill, and in a moment, it was buzzing in joyful circles around the man's head. As it flew away, it said, "Thank you, sir. I won't forget your kindness."

Later that afternoon, the man felt dry and dusty, so he stopped to have a drink. Just as he lifted the gourd to his lips, he heard a deep voice coming from the grass behind him.

"Water. Just a sip. So thirsty—so thirsty."

The man turned around and jumped back when he saw a large, mud-caked crocodile, its tongue hanging out between its long, sharp teeth.

"Help," croaked the crocodile. "Lost my way. Need drink—now."

"Open wide," said the man. "I'll give you a drink."

He poured most of the water into the huge mouth. The crocodile gulped noisily.

"Thanks," it rasped. "Won't forget your kindness." Then, it slowly crawled away.

As the man walked along, he saw a man standing on the side of a hill, so he climbed up to talk to him.

"Good day to you," said the stranger. "Have you come to try to win the hand of the princess?"

The poor man was puzzled. "The princess?" he asked. "What princess?"

"Why," said the stranger, "she is the daughter of the king, of course. He is a very rich king, and his palace is just on the other side of this hill. And, today, the man who can pick the princess out of a crowd of people will have her for his bride."

"That doesn't sound very difficult," replied the man.

"Oh, but it's not as easy as it sounds," said the stranger, "for the princess has lived in a faraway city all her life. No one has ever seen her, so no one knows what she looks like."

The man thanked the stranger and climbed to the top of the hill. From there, he saw a large village and a magnificent palace.

The man hurried down the hill. The village was packed with people. How could he ever move around and see all the young girls? What would a princess look like, anyway? And, he thought, looking down at his dusty, shabby clothes, even if he could pick her out, she wouldn't want him.

The young man felt hot and bothered, and there was an insect buzzing around his head that he couldn't get rid of. Suddenly, he heard a familiar voice.

"Don't worry," it piped, "it's only me, the bee you helped a few days ago. Now, it's my turn to help you. Watch me. I'll fly to a girl and buzz around her. She'll throw her arms in the air to brush me away. Go and take her to the king—she is the princess."

Before the man had time to thank the bee, it flew into the crowd. In a moment, he saw a girl frantically waving her arms about. The man saw that she was very beautiful. He hesitated, and then he went up to her and said, "You are the king's daughter."

The girl nodded, and the word went through the crowd. Then, the king came up, but when he saw how poor the man was, he said, "Yes, you have chosen my daughter, but there are many tasks you must complete before you can marry her. There is a heap of mixed seeds in my courtyard. By morning, you must separate the millet and the maize into separate piles."

The man saw that the hill of seeds filled nearly half the courtyard. He sighed and shook his head. How could he possibly do it in just one night?

Just then, a small bird alighted on his shoulder. "Hello, friend," it said. "Can I be of any help?"

The man was delighted to see the weaverbird again. He told the bird about the task the king had given him. The bird chirped, "I'll be back in a minute. Don't go away."

The man wondered what the little bird was up to. Then, he saw what looked like a gray cloud above the palace roof, moving toward him. It was hundreds of weaverbirds, all heading for the courtyard. They dived into

the pile and picked up the seeds, one by one, in their beaks.

"We're good at this sort of thing," said the weaverbird. And, by morning, they had separated the seeds into two big piles. As they flew off over the palace roof, the man shouted, "Thank you!"

When the king saw the seeds separated into two neat piles, he muttered, "Indeed, yes . . . yes . . . well, you have completed the first task, but there will be another one this evening."

When the man went to the palace in the evening, the king told him to sit at a table. Then, four servants came out of the kitchen, carrying a platter with an entire roasted bull. When the servants put the platter down, the table groaned under its weight.

The king sneered and said, "You must eat all the meat of this cooked bull by morning, right down to the bones."

The man chewed a few mouthfuls, and because he was hungry, he thought it would be easy enough to eat all the meat. But soon, he felt stuffed, and he couldn't face another bite, though there was still a mountain of meat before him.

All of a sudden, he saw the bright eyes of an animal creeping toward him. He looked around for a place to hide, but then he heard a familiar voice.

"Don't be frightened, kind sir. It's only me, the hyena you fed out on the plains. What are you doing here?"

As the man explained his impossible task, a big smile spread across the hyena's face. "Allow me to fetch my family," said the hyena. "We will have no trouble dealing with this little problem of yours."

The hyena returned in a few minutes with its hungry family, and they wasted no time in digging in and tearing off every bit of meat.

The next morning, the king was astonished to see a pile of bones where the bull had been, and the platter licked clean. "You have completed the second task," he growled, "but this afternoon, you shall face the final task."

The king was sure that the man could not succeed with this last task. In the marketplace, the king announced to all the people, "To win my daughter's hand, this man must cross the river in broad daylight and bring back the magical ostrich feather from the far side of the river."

At once, the crowd fell silent. When the young man looked across the river, he saw why. In the water, he saw the bulging eyes and lashing tails of hundreds of hungry crocodiles.

The man could not move. If he went forward, he would certainly be killed. If he went backward, he would lose the king's daughter, who stood farther up the bank, gazing at him with admiring eyes.

A deep voice interrupted his thoughts. "Down here. At your feet. Got a problem?"

There was the crocodile he had helped, looking much happier than before. The man explained his final task.

"No problem," said the crocodile. "Kind man. You'll see." Then, with a swish of its tail, it disappeared underwater.

The man stared as the crocodiles formed a straight line across the river, each crocodile holding the tail of the one in front.

"Step across," said the man's friend. "Bridge of crocodiles."

As the man stepped onto the crocodile's back, the crowd started to clap and shout. He walked faster and faster over the living bridge until he reached the other side. He picked up the ostrich feather and hurried back across the bridge of crocodiles. When he stepped off, he thanked his crocodile friend.

"Any time," said the crocodile, and it sank back under the water.

The people crowded around the young man and clapped and cheered as he made his way to the king and his daughter.

The king said, "You may be dressed in rags, but you have a noble heart. Welcome to my family."

The princess smiled, and the poor man knew that his lonely days were gone forever. ❧

THE POOR MAN'S REWARD

The Water of Life

adapted from the Brothers Grimm

There once was a king who fell very ill. The royal doctors examined him and frowned and shook their heads. They went to the king's three sons and said, "Alas, we have given your father our most powerful medicines, but day by day he grows weaker. There is nothing more we can do. Your royal father, we fear, has little time to live."

The three sons were saddened by this news, and they went down into the palace garden and wept.

Just then, an old man passed by. When he saw the three young princes in tears, he stopped to ask, "Young masters, why do you grieve? You are in the flower of youth, when your voices should ring with laughter. What brings these tears from your eyes?"

They told him their father was so ill that he would most certainly die, for nothing seemed to cure him. Then, the old man said, "I know of one remedy, and that is the water of life. If he drinks it, he will become well again. But, it is hard to find, and the way is filled with danger."

The oldest son said, "I will find it," and he went to the sick king. "Father," he said, "I beg you to let me go forth in search of the water of life, for that alone can save you."

"No," said the king, "the danger is too great. I would rather die."

But, the oldest son begged so long that the king at last consented.

"I will not fail you, my father," said the oldest prince. "I would do anything to save your life." But, in his heart he thought, "If I bring the water of life, then I shall be best beloved of my father, and I alone shall inherit the kingdom."

So, he set out, and when he had ridden forth a little distance, he came across a dwarf by the side of the road, who called to him and said, "Where do you ride so fast, young master?"

"Silly shrimp," said the prince very haughtily, "it is nothing to you." And, he spurred his horse and rode on, leaving the dwarf in a cloud of dust.

The dwarf grew angry, and, staring hard at the prince, he wished an evil wish.

Soon, the prince entered a narrow valley. The farther he rode, the closer the mountains drew together. At last, the road became so narrow that he could not advance another step. It was impossible either to turn his horse or to dismount from the saddle, and he was shut in as if in prison.

THE WATER OF LIFE

The sick king waited long for his oldest son to return, but he did not come. Then, the second son said, "Father, let me go forth to seek the water of life, for that alone can save you." But, he thought to himself, "If my brother is dead, then the kingdom will be mine."

At first, the king would not allow him to go, but at last he agreed, so the prince set out on the same road that his brother had taken. Soon, 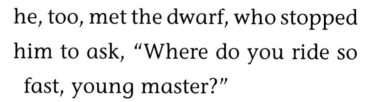 he, too, met the dwarf, who stopped him to ask, "Where do you ride so fast, young master?"

"Silly pipsqueak," said the prince, "it is none of your business," and he rode on without giving the dwarf another look.

But, the dwarf stared after him and wished an evil wish. And, before long, the prince went into a forest. As he rode, the way grew thick with thorns and vines, till at last he found himself trapped and could go neither forward nor backward.

As the second son also remained away so long, the youngest begged to be allowed to go forth to fetch the water. At last, the king agreed to let him go. "But, only return," said the king, "when you have found your brothers and can bring them home with you."

"I shall do as you wish, father," said the youngest son.

On the road, he met the dwarf, who stopped him to ask, "Where do you ride so fast, young master?"

The young prince stopped his horse and dismounted. "Greetings to you, sir," he said. "I ride to seek the water of life, for my father is sick, and without it, he shall surely die."

"A gentle answer, and true," said the dwarf. "But, do you know where this water is to be found?"

"No," admitted the prince. "But, I shall seek until I find it, for my father's sake."

"You speak well," said the dwarf, "not like your haughty brothers who answer with insults. I will tell you how to obtain the water of life.

It springs from a fountain in the courtyard of an enchanted castle. Take this iron wand, and with it strike three times on the iron door of the castle, and it will spring open. Inside lie two lions with gaping jaws and sharp teeth. Take these two loaves of bread, and throw a loaf to each of them, and they will be quieted. Then hurry to fetch some of the water of life before the clock strikes twelve, else the door will shut again and you will be locked in forever."

The prince took the wand and the bread and warmly thanked the dwarf, and then set out on his way. When he arrived at the enchanted castle, everything was as the dwarf had said. The door sprang open at the third stroke of the wand. As the prince entered, the lions stirred and roared, but to each he tossed a loaf of bread, and the beasts lay down to chew like contented kittens.

The prince entered the castle and came to a large and splendid hall. There sat a beautiful maiden who rejoiced when she saw him. "Long have I waited for you," she said. "You shall have the whole of my kingdom, and if you return in a year, our wedding shall be celebrated. But first, as I know, you must bring the water of life to your father." And, she told him where to find the spring where the water flowed. "It is far," she said, "and you must hurry to draw some of it before the clock strikes twelve."

The prince thanked her and hurried on, until at last he came to the spring. He drew some water in a cup and hastened away. He heard the clock striking a quarter to twelve and ran as fast as he could. Just as the clock struck twelve, he leaped through the opening, and the iron door fell with such force that it cut away a piece of his boot.

"I have the water of life!" the prince rejoiced. On his way homeward, he again passed the dwarf. "Kind dwarf," said the prince, "can you tell me where my two brothers are? They went out before I did in search of the water of life, and have not returned."

"One is imprisoned between two mountains," said the dwarf, "and the other is trapped in vines and thorns. I have condemned them to stay there, because they were so haughty."

But, the prince pleaded until at last the dwarf agreed to release the brothers. "But," said the dwarf, "I warn you, beware of them, for they have bad hearts."

When the prince found his brothers, he rejoiced, and told them how he had found the water of life, and had brought a cupful with him. He also told them how he had found a beautiful princess who was willing to wait a year for him, and then their wedding would be celebrated, and he would rule a great kingdom.

After that, they rode on together. During the journey, the two older brothers rode apart and whispered to each other, "Our younger brother has found the water of life, and for that our father will give him the kingdom— the kingdom that belongs to us!" They then began to plot with each other how to ruin their brother. They waited until they found him fast asleep, and then they poured the water of life out of his cup and into theirs, and took the water for themselves. Into his cup, they poured salty seawater.

When they arrived home, the youngest son took his cup to the sick king so that he could drink and be cured. But, scarcely had the king drunk a very little bit of the salty seawater than he became still worse than before.

Then, the two older brothers came to the king. "Our younger brother has tried to poison you," they claimed. "Here, father, drink this." And, they handed him the cup with the true water of life. The king sipped it and felt his sickness departing, and he became strong and healthy as in the days of his youth.

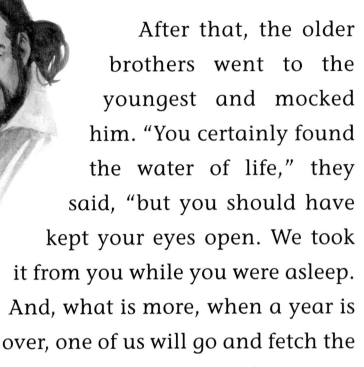

After that, the older brothers went to the youngest and mocked him. "You certainly found the water of life," they said, "but you should have kept your eyes open. We took it from you while you were asleep. And, what is more, when a year is over, one of us will go and fetch the beautiful princess who has promised to marry you. And, it will do you no good to try to tell our father, for he is so angry that he has banished you from the kingdom. You must leave and be a wanderer all your days, for if you stay, you shall lose your life."

With bitter tears, the prince set off from the palace, thinking that he would never again see his home or his beloved father.

And, he wandered through forest and valley, over mountain and plain. The days turned to weeks, and the weeks to months, till almost a year had passed.

In the meantime, the princess had ordered that a road be made to her castle. This was no ordinary road of stones and gravel, but a road all bright and golden. And, the princess told her guards that whoever came riding to her straight up the middle of the road should be allowed to enter the castle, but whoever rode by the side of the road should be sent away.

Almost a year had passed since the princess met the youngest son. Now, the eldest son decided to go to the princess, claim her for his bride, and take her kingdom for his own. So, he rode forth, and when he came near the castle, he saw the splendid golden road. "It would be a great shame," he thought, "if I were to ride over so valuable a road, and lose even one fragment of this gold." So, he turned his horse and rode just to the right side of the road. But, when he came to the door, the guards would not allow him to enter, and told him to go away.

Soon after this, the second prince set out, and when he came to the golden road, and his horse had put one foot on it, he thought, "It would be a shame to ride on this valuable road and break off even a piece of it." So, he turned his horse and rode just to the left side of the road. When he reached the door, the guards told him to go away.

It was now a year to the day since the youngest prince had left the enchanted castle where he had met the princess and found the water of life. And, on this day, his wanderings brought him again near the castle. His head was full of thoughts of the princess. So much did he wish to be with her that as he walked, he never noticed the golden road at all. So, he walked straight up the middle of the golden road, and when he came to the door, it was opened, and the princess received him with joy.

THE WATER OF LIFE

"You have returned," she said, "as I trusted you would do." And so, their wedding was celebrated with great rejoicing.

"I have such happiness," said the prince, "that it seems selfish to wish for more. Yet, I would wish that my father could know of our marriage and share in our joy."

"I shall go to him," said the princess.

And so, she rode to the palace of the king, and told him how the older brothers had betrayed the youngest, and all else that had passed. The old king wished to punish them, but they had fled from the land, and they never came back as long as they lived. ❧

The Wonderful Brocade

a legend from China

Along time ago in China, in a wide, green valley surrounded by mountains, there lived an old woman who wove the most wonderful brocades the world had ever seen. On pieces of smooth silk, she wove threads of gold, silver, and other colors into pictures that seemed to come to life. When she wove a tiger, it seemed to leap out from the cloth. When she wove a flower, it seemed to bloom in the sunshine. And, when she wove a crane, it looked so real and so alive that it seemed ready to fly away.

Each week, the old woman sold her brocades in the village, and with the money she received, she bought food for her three sons, as well as needles and silken thread for her weavings. Then one day, as she walked through the village, she saw a painting in a merchant's shop. The painting showed a tall castle, surrounded by gardens full of flowers and vegetables, with a shining river flowing nearby.

"Never, even in my dreams, have I seen a place so beautiful," she sighed. And, instead of buying food and needles and silken thread, she gave the merchant all but a few of her pennies to buy the painting.

When she returned home, two of her sons were already sitting at the table, each with a small pile of twigs at his feet. The old woman unrolled the painting on the table before them and said, "Wouldn't it be wonderful if we could live in this castle?"

"Mother!" cried the oldest son. "How foolish of you to buy such a thing. We will never live in so grand a place as that."

"What about our rice?" whined the second son. "We will have to cut more wood to buy food, and my hands are sore already!"

Just then, the door opened, and the youngest son entered, carrying on his back a satchel bulging with wood.

When he saw the painting, he cried, "How beautiful!" Then, he noticed his mother's sorrowful face. "Ah-mee," he said gently, "why do you look so sad?"

"Oh, my son," she sighed, "I want so much to live in a place like that, so beautiful and peaceful."

The youngest son thought for a moment and said, "Why don't you weave a copy of it? While you weave, you will feel like you live there. And, your weavings look so real that when you are finished, we will feel like we live there, too."

The old woman clapped her hands in delight, gathered her most beautiful thread, and sat down in front of her loom.

Day after day, week after week, month after month, the old woman did nothing but weave a copy of the beautiful painting. She rarely ate and rarely slept. When the smoke from the lamp burned her eyes, her tears dropped onto the threads, but she did not stop—instead, she wove the tears into the threads of the shining river and the sparkling fishpond. And, at the end of the second year, when drops of blood dripped from her cracked fingers onto the threads, she still did not stop, but wove them into scarlet flower petals and the glow of the setting sun.

At last, at the end of the third year, she finished her weaving. The castle walls glowed, and the flowers seemed to bloom in the sunshine. When she spread out the cloth before her sons, all three of them stood still and admired it.

While they gazed, a playful breeze swept into the room and tickled the edges of the brocade. Then, a puff of wind pushed between them, lifted up the wonderful brocade, and carried it out the window.

"Stop! Stop!" cried the sons to the invisible thief. They chased the brocade across the valley, but the wind always held it just out of their reach. At last, with one great gust, it blew the brocade over the mountains and disappeared.

When the young men went back to the cottage, they found their mother lying on the doorstep. As they gently carried her inside to her bed, she whispered, "Oh, my sons, you must bring me back my wonderful brocade. I have put my life into it. My heart will break, and I fear I will die if it is not returned."

The oldest son boasted, "I am the only one who can bring the brocade back to you, Ah-mee. My brothers are too young for such an important task. But, do not fear, I will have your brocade back to you by morning."

Then, he strode out the door and climbed the mountains without stopping until he reached the narrow pass that led to the lands to the east. There, he noticed to one side a little stone hut and a wrinkled old man sitting on the doorstep.

"Good afternoon," croaked the old man. "Where are you going on such a fine day?"

"I am going to find my mother's brocade, which the wind has stolen away."

"Ah," said the old man, "the wind serves the fairies of the Sun Palace. You will find your mother's weaving there. But, it will not be easy. To reach the Sun Palace, you will have to pass through the Valley of Fire and the Sea of Ice. If you cry out even once in the Valley of Fire, you will be turned into a pile of ash. And, if you so much as shiver as you pass through the Sea of Ice, you will be turned to ice forever."

The oldest son's teeth chattered, and his face paled. He was proud, but he was not brave. The old man shook his head and said, "There is another way." He held out a small box, full of gold coins. "Take this," he said, "and do as you will."

The oldest son snatched the box out of the old man's hands, and, without a word of thanks, ran away down the mountain. He was too ashamed to go home, so he went to live in the city.

When the oldest son did not return, the second son said, "I suppose now I must go and try to find your wonderful brocade, Ah-mee."

With much groaning and moaning, he climbed the mountains to the narrow pass. Like his brother, he met the wrinkled old man at the little stone hut. And, like his brother, he chose the box of gold and ran away to live in the city.

As the weeks passed, the old woman grew weaker. At last, the youngest son said, "Ah-mee, please let me go to find your wonderful brocade. Our neighbors will care for you while I am gone."

The old woman nodded weakly, and the youngest son set off at once, east through the mountains toward the rising sun. When he reached the little stone hut by the narrow mountain pass, the old man said, "Good afternoon, my friend. Where are you going on such a fine day?"

"I am going to find my mother's brocade, which the wind has stolen away."

"The wind serves the fairies of the Sun Palace. You will find your mother's weaving there."

"Thank you," cried the youngest son, "I will go there at once!"

THE WONDERFUL BROCADE

"But wait, my bold young friend," said the old man. "To reach the Sun Palace, you will have to pass through the Valley of Fire and the Sea of Ice. If you cry out even once in the Valley of Fire, you will be turned into a pile of ash. If you so much as shiver as you pass through the Sea of Ice, you will be turned to ice forever."

The young man thought for a moment and said, "Then, for my mother's sake, I must not cry out, and I must not shiver."

"There is another way," croaked the old man. He held out another small box filled with gold coins. "Take this, and do as you will."

"Thank you," replied the youngest son, "but gold will not heal my mother's heart. She needs her brocade, and I am the only one left who can bring it to her."

The old man smiled. "I will lend you my horse," he said. "If you do not cry out and you do not shiver, he will carry you safely to the Sun Palace."

Then, he took two stone teeth out of his pocket and put them into the mouth of a stone horse that stood by the hut. The horse shook, stretched, and trotted to the youngest son's side. Then, the young man leaped onto the stone horse's back and galloped through the narrow pass.

The stone horse raced down the mountain and into the Valley of Fire. Flames rose all around the young man. They snapped at his face and clothes. But, he remembered his mother working at her loom, and for her sake, he did not cry out.

After they crossed the Valley of Fire, the young man hardly had time to take a breath before the stone horse plunged into the Sea of Ice. But, when the waves crashed over him, he remembered his mother's tears, and for her sake, he did not shiver.

At last, the greatest of the freezing waves rose up before them. The youngest son closed his eyes, crouched close to the horse's strong stone neck, and held on tight as they burst through the wall of water.

When the young man looked up again, the bronze towers of the Sun Palace stood before him. He jumped down from the stone horse and ran into the castle, searching for his mother's wonderful brocade.

As he was searching, he turned a corner and found himself in a beautiful room where 12 lovely fairies sat weaving at 12 looms. Each fairy was weaving a copy of his mother's wonderful brocade, which hung from the center of the ceiling.

But, when the fairies saw the youngest son, their songs and laughter stopped, and they looked at him with frightened eyes.

"Please," he said, "do not be afraid. I have come for my mother's brocade. I fear she will die if I do not return it to her quickly."

The loveliest of the fairies stepped forward and replied, "We do not wish any harm to come to your mother. We only took the brocade because it was so wonderful that we wanted to make copies of it ourselves. Certainly you may have it back. But, may we keep it one last night so that we might finish our weavings?"

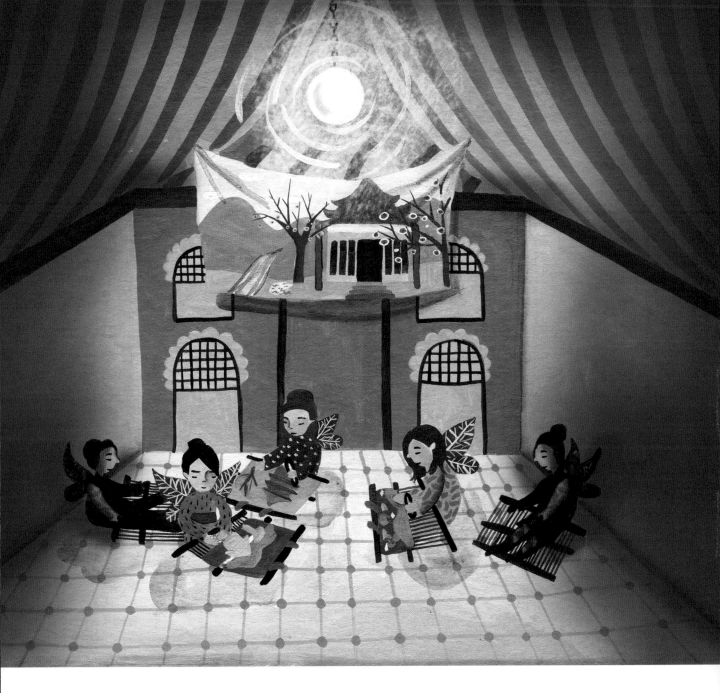

The youngest son agreed, and the loveliest fairy invited him to sit in a chair of carved jade, and offered him delicious food to eat. As the sky grew dark, the fairies hung up a large pearl and worked by the light of its glow.

The loveliest fairy was the first to finish her weaving. But, it was not nearly as beautiful as the old woman's. She looked at the sleeping young man and at the weaving and thought, "I wish that I, too, could live in such a beautiful place." Then, quietly, she took up her needle and silk thread and stitched a picture of herself sitting by the fishpond in the old woman's weaving.

When the sun rose, the last of the fairies finished her work. Then, the fairies rolled up the brocade and gave it back to the youngest son. He thanked them, sprang upon the horse's back, and galloped to the wrinkled old man's little stone hut in the mountains.

"You are brave, my boy," he croaked, "but now you must be swift. Your mother is dying. Put on these boots of mine, and they will hurry you home."

The young man put on the boots, and in two steps, he was standing at his front door.

"Ah-mee," he shouted, running inside, "Ah-mee! I have it! I have your wonderful brocade."

The old woman's eyes opened. With one hand, she reached out to touch her son's face. With the other, she took the brocade and held it to her heart.

"Let us look at it in the sunlight," said the youngest son, and he gently helped his mother out of bed.

Outside, it was a beautiful day. The birds were singing and the sun was shining. Under the clear blue sky, the old woman began to unroll the brocade.

But to their surprise, as the brocade unrolled, it grew larger and larger. The flowers and trees the old woman had woven took root in the ground. The animals leaped up from their places in the cloth and frisked among the fields. And, in a moment, the tall castle stood where their thatched cottage had been, and the shining river flowed at their feet.

They were even more amazed when they saw the loveliest fairy sitting by the fishpond. And before long, as you might have guessed, the fairy and the youngest son were married, and together with the old woman, they lived happily in the castle by the shining river.

One day, many years later, two beggars wandered past the castle garden. It was the two brothers, but they had spent all their gold and had nothing left. They saw their mother and their brother with his wife and children walking and laughing together among the trees. Too ashamed to call out to them, the brothers tiptoed away, never to return.

THE WONDERFUL BROCADE

The *Pine Tree* and
Its Needles

A little pine tree lived in the woods. It had leaves like long green needles. But, the little pine tree was not happy.

"I do not like my green needles," it said. "I wish I had beautiful leaves. How happy I should be if only I had gold leaves!"

Night came. Then, the Fairy of the Trees walked in the woods. "Little pine tree," she said, "you may have your wish."

In the morning, the little pine tree had leaves of gold.

"How beautiful I am!" it said. "See how I shine in the sun! Now, I am happy!"

Night came. Then, a man walked in the woods. He took all the gold leaves and put them into a bag. The little tree had no leaves at all.

"What shall I do?" it said. "I do not want gold leaves again. I wish I had glass leaves. Glass leaves would shine in the sun, too. And, no one would take glass leaves."

Night came. The Fairy walked in the woods again.

"Little pine tree," she said, "you may have your wish."

In the morning, the tree had glass leaves. "How beautiful I am!" it said. "See how I shine in the sun! Now, I am happy."

Night came. Then, the wind came through the woods. Oh, how it blew! It broke all the beautiful glass leaves.

"What shall I do now?" said the tree. "I do not want glass leaves again. The oak tree has big green leaves. I wish I had big green leaves, too."

Night came. Then, the Fairy of the Trees walked in the woods again. "Little pine tree," she said, "you may have your wish."

In the morning, the little pine tree had big green leaves. "How beautiful I am!" it said. "Now, I am like the other trees. At last, I am happy."

Night came. A goat came through the woods. He ate all the big green leaves.

"What shall I do?" said the tree. "A man took my leaves of gold. The wind broke my leaves of glass. A goat ate my big green leaves. I wish I had my long needles again."

Night came. The Fairy walked in the woods again.

"Little pine tree," she said, "you may have your wish."

In the morning, the little pine tree had its long needles again.

"Now, I am happy," said the tree. "I do not want any other leaves. Little pine needles are best for little pine trees."

The *Little Rabbit Who Wanted Red Wings*

an American folktale retold by Betty Erickson

Little Rabbit had soft white fur, long pink ears, shiny red eyes, and a puffy tail. But, he didn't like the way he looked.

When Squirrel raced by, Little Rabbit wished for Squirrel's big, bushy tail. When he saw Porcupine's pointy quills, he wished he had quills. When Duck waddled by, he wished for her floppy orange feet, too.

Little Rabbit kept on wishing. But, his mother said, "I love you just the way you are."

One day, Groundhog heard Little Rabbit wishing and said, "Go to the Wishing Pond and look at yourself in the water. Turn around three times and make a wish."

So, Little Rabbit hopped to the Wishing Pond. He saw himself in the pond and turned around three times.

He sat down to think of a wish. While he was thinking, a red bird came by for a drink. Little Rabbit saw the bird and wished for red wings.

Suddenly, he could feel wings beginning to grow. The wings grew and grew.

Then, Little Rabbit went off to show his mother his red wings. "Mother Rabbit! I'm home," he called. But, Mother Rabbit didn't know him, as she had never seen a rabbit with red wings.

It was getting dark, so Little Rabbit asked Porcupine if he could spend the night with him. But, Porcupine didn't know him either.

Little Rabbit was tired and cold and hungry. He sat down on the path and cried. Groundhog found him and took him home for the night.

The next morning, Little Rabbit tried out  his wings, but they didn't work. He got caught in a sticker bush, and Groundhog had to get him out.

"Don't you like your beautiful red wings?" Groundhog asked.

"No!" Little Rabbit cried. "No!"

"Then, go back to the Wishing Pond and make a wish," Groundhog said.

So, Little Rabbit hurried to the Wishing Pond. He saw himself in the pond. He turned around three times and wished to be himself again. Suddenly, the red wings disappeared. Then, he went home as fast as he could hop.

His mother said, "My Little Rabbit, you are home at last."

And, he never went back to the Wishing Pond again. ❧

The *The* **Country Mouse** *and the* **City Mouse**

Once there was a mouse. She lived in the country.

One day, her cousin came to see her. Her cousin lived in the city.

The Country Mouse was very glad to see the City Mouse and asked her to stay for dinner.

"Thank you," said the City Mouse. And, she took off her hat and coat, and helped put the dishes on the table.

When dinner was ready, the City Mouse looked at the corn and the beans, and said to herself, "What a funny dinner! Not a bit of cake or cheese."

"Come to my house," she said. "I have cheese every day for my dinner."

"Thank you very much," said the Country Mouse. "I'll go."

So, the two mice went to the city. When they got there, they were very hungry. "Come to the kitchen," said the City Mouse. "I'll show you where the cook keeps the things."

The City Mouse ran across the kitchen and into a big closet. "The cook made a pie," she said. "I must find it."

She looked around in the closet until she found the pie. "Here it is," said the City Mouse. "This is better than corn and beans."

Just as they were beginning to eat, they heard a terrible noise in the kitchen. "What's that?" asked the Country Mouse.

"That's the cat," whispered the City Mouse. "Run!"

Both mice ran. When they were safe, the Country Mouse asked, "Why did you run?"

"Never stay in the kitchen when the cat comes," said the City Mouse. "She would eat you up. We will go to the cellar and find some apples. I like apples."

So, away the two mice went to the nice, cool cellar.

"What a lot of apples!" said the Country Mouse. "And, there is a big pot of soup. Do you smell cheese? I do."

"Yes, I smell cheese," said the City Mouse, "but we won't eat it. It is in a trap."

"What is a trap?" asked the Country Mouse.

The City Mouse showed her the trap. "The cook puts cheese in it," said the City Mouse, "but if you eat the cheese, something comes down hard on your head and kills you."

The Country Mouse looked at the trap. "I will go home," she said. "I do not like your house. There is a cat in the kitchen and a trap in the cellar. I like my corn and beans better than your pie and apples." &

The Cap that Mother Made

adapted from Carolyn Sherwin Bailey

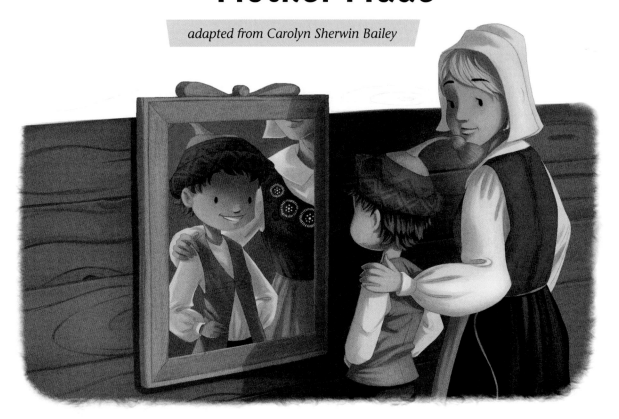

Once there was a boy named Anders who had a new cap. A nicer cap you have never seen. His mother had made it, and no one can make anything as nice as a mother can. It was a red cap, except for a small part in the middle. That was green, for there had not been enough red yarn to make the whole cap. A blue tassel sat on top.

The very first day Anders got his cap, he put it on. Next, he walked around his house for a while. He wanted his brothers and sisters to see how good he looked in it. Then, he put his hands in his pockets and went for a walk outside. He wanted everyone to see his fine new cap.

Soon, he met a farmer coming down the road. The farmer was driving a wagon full of wood. When the farmer saw Anders's new cap, he made a bow. He bowed so deeply that his head nearly touched the ground.

"Well, well, if it isn't my friend Anders," the farmer said. "At first, I thought you were a prince or a duke in such a fine new cap. Let me wear it for a while, and I'll give you a ride in my wagon."

Anders just smiled and shook his head. A ride in a wagon would be nice, but not as nice as a cap made by his mother. He walked down the road, holding his head high.

THE CAP THAT MOTHER MADE

At a turn in the road, he met Lars, the clock maker's son. Lars was a big boy who wore high boots and carried a pocketknife. His eyes grew wide when he saw Anders's new cap.

"Let's trade caps," said Lars. "I'll even give you my pocketknife, too."

Now, this knife was a good one, though half the blade was gone and the handle was cracked. Anders thought that he would like to have that knife. But, it was not as wonderful as a cap made by his own mother.

"No, thanks," said Anders. He nodded good-bye to Lars and went on his way.

Next, Anders met a little old lady who smiled and curtsied until her dress looked like a balloon.

"My, you look handsome in that new cap," she said. "You look like you're dressed for the royal ball."

"Yes, why not?" thought Anders. "My cap is so fine, I may as well go see the king."

So, off he went to see the king.

At the palace door, he met two soldiers with shining helmets and guns on their shoulders.

"Where do you think you are going, my boy?" one soldier asked.

"I am going to the royal ball," Anders told them.

"No, you are not," said the other soldier, stepping forward. "Nobody can go to the royal ball unless he's dressed in a uniform."

Just then, the princess came running across the palace yard. She was dressed in a white silk gown with ribbons of gold.

"It's true this boy has no uniform," she said. "But, look at his fine new cap. That will do just as well as a uniform."

So, the princess took Anders by the hand, and into the palace they went.

Anders and the princess walked through gleaming halls and shining rooms. Wherever they went, smiling ladies and gentlemen bowed. They must have thought Anders was a prince in his fine new cap.

At the end of the longest hall stood a table set with golden cups and plates. Piles of cakes and candy filled silver dishes.

The princess sat down at the long table. She let Anders sit in a golden chair by her side.

"But, you must not eat with your cap on," she said. She put out her hand to take off the cap.

"Oh yes, I can eat just as well with it on," said Anders. He held on to his cap. He thought that if he took it off, people would no longer believe he was a prince. Besides, he was not sure he would get it back.

"Well, if you give it to me, I will give you a kiss," said the princess.

The princess was very beautiful. Anders thought he would like a kiss from her. But, he would not give up the cap his mother made for anything. He only shook his head.

Then, the princess filled his pockets with cakes. She put her own gold chain around his neck. She bent down and kissed him.

"Now, will you give me the cap?" she asked.

Anders moved back in his chair. Not once did he take his hands from his head.

Just then, the doors flew open, and in came the king himself. He wore a great purple robe that trailed behind him, and he had a large gold crown on his curly white hair.

He smiled when he saw Anders sitting in the golden chair.

"That is a very fine cap you have," said the king.

"So it is," said Anders. "My mother made it for me, and everyone wants to get it."

"But, surely you would like to change caps with me," said the king. He raised his gold crown from his head.

Anders never said a word. He sat very still, holding on to his cap. The king came near with his gold crown in one hand and his other hand stretching to grab Anders's cap. With one jump, Anders was out of his chair. He darted like an arrow down the long hall.

Anders twisted like an eel between the arms of all those fine ladies and gentlemen. He jumped like a rabbit past the soldiers at the palace gate.

He ran so fast that the princess's necklace flew off his neck and all the cakes fell out of his pockets. But, he held on to his cap. He was still holding on to it with both hands as he rushed into his cottage.

"Hello, Anders. Where have you been?" asked his mother. Anders climbed into her lap and told her all that had happened. His brothers and sisters stood around and listened with their mouths open.

"You silly boy," cried his big brother. "Why didn't you trade your cap for the king's gold crown? Just think how much money you could get for a crown. You could buy a whole house full of caps."

Anders had not thought of that, and his face turned as red as a tomato. He put his arms around his mother's neck.

"Mother, was I silly?" he asked.

His mother hugged him and kissed him.

"No, my boy," she said. "If you were dressed in silver and gold from top to toe, you could not look any nicer than you do in your little red cap."

Then, Anders felt fine again. He knew that the cap his mother made was the best cap in the world. ❧

The **Camel** and the **Pig**

One day, a camel and a pig were talking. The camel was proud because he was tall. But, the pig was proud because he was short.

"Just look at me!" said the camel. "See how tall I am! It is better to be tall, like me."

"Oh, no!" said the pig. "Just look at me! See how short I am! It is better to be short, like me."

"If I am not right, I will give up my hump," said the camel.

"If I am not right, I will give up my snout," said the pig.

Soon, they came to a garden. All around it was a wall. There was no gate in the wall.

The camel was so tall that he could see over the wall. He could see fine, ripe fruit in the garden. His neck was so long that he could reach over the wall and get the fruit. He ate all he wanted.

THE CAMEL AND THE PIG

But, the poor pig was short. He could not reach over the wall. He could not get inside, because there was no gate.

"Ha, ha, ha!" laughed the camel. "Now would you rather be tall or short?"

Soon, they came to another garden. All around it was a high wall. It was so high that the camel could not see over it.

But, there was a low gate in the wall. The pig went through the gate.

This garden was full of fine, ripe fruit, too. The pig ate all he wanted.

But, the camel was so tall that he could not get through the low gate.

"Ha, ha, ha!" laughed the pig. "Now would you rather be tall or short?"

So, the camel kept his hump, and the pig kept his snout. For, they said, "It is sometimes better to be tall, and sometimes better to be small."

Heron *and* the **Hummingbird**

a Hitchiti tale retold by S.E. Schlosser

Heron and Hummingbird were very good friends, even though one was tall and gangly and awkward and one was small and sleek and fast. They both loved to eat fish. Hummingbird preferred small fish like minnows, and Heron liked the large ones.

One day, Hummingbird said to his friend, "I am not sure there are enough fish in the world for both of our kind to eat.

Why don't we have a race to see which of us should own the fish?"

Heron thought that was a very good idea. They decided that they would race for four days. The finish line was an old, dead tree next to a faraway river. Whichever of them sat on top of the tree first on the fourth day of the race would own all the fish in the world.

They started out the next morning. Hummingbird zipped along, flying around and around Heron, who was moving steadily forward, flapping his giant wings. Then, Hummingbird would be distracted by the pretty flowers along the way. He would flit from one to the other, tasting the nectar. When Hummingbird noticed that Heron was ahead of him, he hurried to catch up with him, zooming ahead as fast as he could, and leaving Heron far behind. Heron just kept flying steadily forward, flapping his giant wings.

Hummingbird was tired from all his flitting. When it got dark, he decided to rest. He found a nice spot to perch and slept all night long. But, Heron just kept flying steadily forward all night long, flapping his giant wings.

When Hummingbird woke in the morning, Heron was far ahead. Hummingbird had to fly as fast as he could to catch up. He zoomed past the big, awkward Heron and kept going until Heron had disappeared behind him. Then, Hummingbird noticed some pretty flowers nearby. He zip-zipped over to them and tasted their nectar. He was enjoying the pretty scenery and didn't notice Heron flap-flapping past him with his great wings.

Hummingbird finally remembered that he was racing with Heron, and he flew as fast as he could to catch up with the big, awkward bird. Then, he zipped along, flying around and around Heron, who kept moving steadily forward, flapping his giant wings.

For two more days, Hummingbird and Heron raced toward the far-distant riverbank with the dead tree that was the finish line.

Hummingbird had a marvelous time sipping nectar and flitting among the flowers and resting himself at night. Heron stoically kept up a steady flap-flapping of his giant wings, propelling himself forward through the air all day and all night.

Hummingbird woke from his sleep the morning of the fourth day, feeling refreshed and invigorated. He zip-zipped toward the riverbank with the dead tree. When it came into view, he saw Heron perched at the top of the tree! Heron had won the race by flying straight and steady through the night while Hummingbird slept.

So, from that day forward, Heron has owned all the fish in the rivers and lakes, and Hummingbird has sipped from the nectar of the many flowers that he enjoyed so much during the race. ❧

The **Tortoise** and the **Hare**

Once there was a hare that lived in a meadow. He liked to hop fast. "Look at me!" he said. "I can hop faster than any animal in the meadow."

A tortoise lived in the meadow, too. One day, he was creeping to the river for a swim.

"How slow you are!" said the hare. "You cannot hop. You can only creep. Look at me! See how fast I hop!" And, the little hare gave a great hop.

"I am slow," said the tortoise. "But, I am sure. Would you like to run a race with me?"

"Run a race!" cried the hare. "How foolish that would be! I hop, and you creep. How can we run a race?"

"Let us try," said the tortoise. "Let us race to the river. We shall see who gets there first."

"The river is a long way off," said the hare. "But I shall get there before you. Good-bye!"

Off went the hare, *hop! hop! hop!*

Off went the tortoise, *creep, creep, creep.*

Soon, the hare was nearly to the river. It was a warm day. "I will rest a little," he said.

So, the hare rested and ate some leaves. Then, he felt sleepy. "It is very warm," he said. "I will sleep a little. That foolish tortoise is slow. I shall wake up before he creeps here. Then, I can hop to the river. I shall get there long before he comes."

So, the hare went to sleep. The little tortoise came creeping on. He did not stop to eat. He did not stop to sleep. He went on and on, *creep, creep, creep.* By and by, he came to the river.

The hare slept a long time. Then, he woke up with a jump. "Dear me! I must hop along," he said. "Where can that slow tortoise be? He is not here yet."

The hare hopped on to the river. But, who was there waiting for him? The tortoise!

Over *in* the Meadow

Over in the meadow,
In the sand, in the sun,
Lived an old mother toad
And her little toadie one.
"Wink!" said the mother;
"I wink," said the one.
So, she winked and she blinked
In the sand, in the sun.

Over in the meadow,
Where the stream runs blue,
Lived an old mother fish
And her little fishes two.
"Swim!" said the mother;
"We swim," said the two.
So, they swam and they leaped
Where the stream runs blue.

Over in the meadow,
In a hole in a tree,
Lived a mother bluebird
And her little bluebirds three.
"Sing!" said the mother;
"We sing," said the three.
So, they sang and were glad
In the hole in the tree.

Over in the meadow,
In the reeds on the shore,
Lived a mother muskrat
And her little muskrats four.
"Dive!" said the mother;
"We dive," said the four.
So, they dived and they burrowed
In the reeds on the shore.

Over in the meadow,
In the snug beehive,
Lived a mother honeybee
And her little honeys five.
"Buzz!" said the mother;
"We buzz," said the five.
So, they buzzed and they hummed
In the snug beehive.

The **Hummingbird** and *the* **Butterfly**

Characters

HUMMINGBIRD
BUTTERFLY

HUMMINGBIRD: Look at that beautiful creature over there! I think I will fly over and say hello.

BUTTERFLY: Hello.

HUMMINGBIRD: Hello. What pretty wings you have! Are you a bird?

BUTTERFLY: No, I am not a bird.

HUMMINGBIRD: What are you?

BUTTERFLY: I am a butterfly.

HUMMINGBIRD: I am a hummingbird. I have pretty wings, just like you. Please come with me. We can fly together. You can be my friend.

BUTTERFLY: No, thank you, Hummingbird. I do not want to go with you. I cannot be your friend.

HUMMINGBIRD: Why not?

BUTTERFLY: You once made fun of me. You said that I was ugly.

HUMMINGBIRD: How can that be true? I have never seen you before. I have never talked to you before. So, I could never have called you ugly. Besides, why would I call you ugly? You are very pretty.

BUTTERFLY: You may not call me ugly now. But, I was once a caterpillar. Then, I did not have pretty wings. You made fun of me. You said I looked like an ugly, furry worm.

HUMMINGBIRD: But, I did not know that someday you would be a butterfly.

BUTTERFLY: That is too bad. You see, even ugly creatures sometimes become beautiful. Good-bye, Hummingbird. I will find other friends.

HUMMINGBIRD: Why?

BUTTERFLY: It is important to be kind to others. It does not matter what they look like.

HUMMINGBIRD: You are right, Butterfly. I am sorry I was mean to you. I am sorry I called you ugly.

BUTTERFLY: I am glad you learned your lesson.

HUMMINGBIRD: Yes. From now on, I will be kind to everyone.

BUTTERFLY: Then, I will fly with you. You can be my friend.

HUMMINGBIRD: We will be good friends. We will be kind to each other. We will be kind to others, too. ❧

The **Lion** and the **Mouse**

adapted from Aesop

Characters

LION

MOUSE

Scene I

LION: (*yawning wide*) I'm so tired after my big meal! I'm going to lie down here to sleep in the sun. I always get sleepy when my

stomach is full. (*yawning again*) A nice nap will do me some good.

MOUSE: (*out of breath*) This ground goes up and down, up and down, hills and valleys, hills and valleys. It's like climbing mountains for my tiny little feet! I need to move to a place that is very, very flat—or one that only goes downhill! Look, here's another big hill. I'll have to climb it to see what's on the other side. (*He climbs up and scampers around on the belly of the sleeping lion.*)

LION: (*in his sleep, like he's dreaming*) Hee-hee. Tee-hee-hee. Stop that! Ha-ha-ha! Stop! (*He shakes his head, opens his eyes, and sees the mouse climbing over his belly.*) Grr! Hey, there! You woke me up. Don't you know it's rude to wake up a lion with tickling? (*trying to swat the little mouse with his paw*) Very rude! I'm going to eat you so you never do that to me again.

THE LION AND THE MOUSE

MOUSE: (*trembling*) Oh, no! Please don't eat me! I didn't know you were alive. I thought you were a hill! It's ruder to eat someone than it is to tickle someone. Please, great King of the Beasts, show mercy to me! If you grant me this favor, I'll never tickle you again when you're sleeping, or even when you're awake. And, I'll never forget that you were kind to me. One day, maybe I can grant you a favor in return.

LION: (*laughing and shaking his head while his belly bounces up and down from his belly laugh*) You're joking. There's nothing you can do for me except add a little flavor to my breakfast. Ha-ha-ha!

MOUSE: (*bouncing up and down on the lion's belly while the lion laughs*) P-p-please don't eat m-m-me! I'm-m-m so t-t-tiny that I won't f-f-fill your st-st-stomach.

LION: That's true. And, when I eat mice, they give me the hiccups. That's worse than being tickled. I'll let you go this time.

Scene II

TWO MONTHS LATER

The lion is caught in a giant net of ropes, lying in the same spot he was in when the mouse first woke him with tickling.

LION: Grr! Help! I'm trapped! Hunters have caught me in this net! Won't someone help me? Grr!

MOUSE: (*looking all around*) What's all that racket? I've been running all day, up and down, up and down, hills and valleys, hills and valleys, and now I hear roaring

like thunder or an earthquake. (*Suddenly, he sees the lion under the net in front of him.*) Oh my! It's that lion again! I need to stay away from this neighborhood.

LION: Help! Grr! Help! Please get me out of this net! When the hunters come back, they'll take me far away!

MOUSE: Well there, King of the Beasts, at least I didn't wake you up this time. What on earth has happened to you? Why are you lying underneath that hammock? For a nap, you should be on top of a hammock, not underneath it.

LION: It's not a hammock! It's a net made of ropes! I'm not napping! I've been trapped by hunters, and I can't break free.

MOUSE: Is that all? Ha-ha-ha. Now, it's my turn to laugh a belly laugh, even if my belly is tiny compared to yours.

LION: That's mean. Why are you laughing? I'm trapped, and I don't know what's going to happen to me.

MOUSE: I'm tiny, but I have good, strong teeth like yours. They're small and sharp. Just watch while I put them to work. Don't be afraid of me, King of the Beasts. I'm not going to tickle you this time.

LION: Stop making fun of me and help me, please. I can't get out of this net.

MOUSE: (*gnawing on one of the ropes in the net; the rope snaps in two*) There! Did you hear that? You weren't dreaming this time. The rope has snapped! (*gnawing on another rope*) There! *Snap!* (*gnawing on a third rope*)

There! *Snap* again! (*gnawing on all the rest of the ropes*) *Snap! Snap! Snap! Snap!* I'm enjoying this. Ha-ha-ha-ha!

LION: (*stretching out his paws and lifting his head*) One by one you have snapped the ropes. You've set me free!

MOUSE: (*laughing*) Ropes can't stop me! You're big, and I'm small—but with my teeth I've snapped them all! See? I told you I might grant you a favor in return one day.

LION: You were right. I'm sorry that I laughed at you before. I see that a tiny little creature like you can do a favor for a great big creature like me. You've taught me that even the smallest friends are important and helpful, and I will never forget your kindness! ॐ